BATMAN TEENAGE MUTANT NINJA TURTLES ADVENTURES

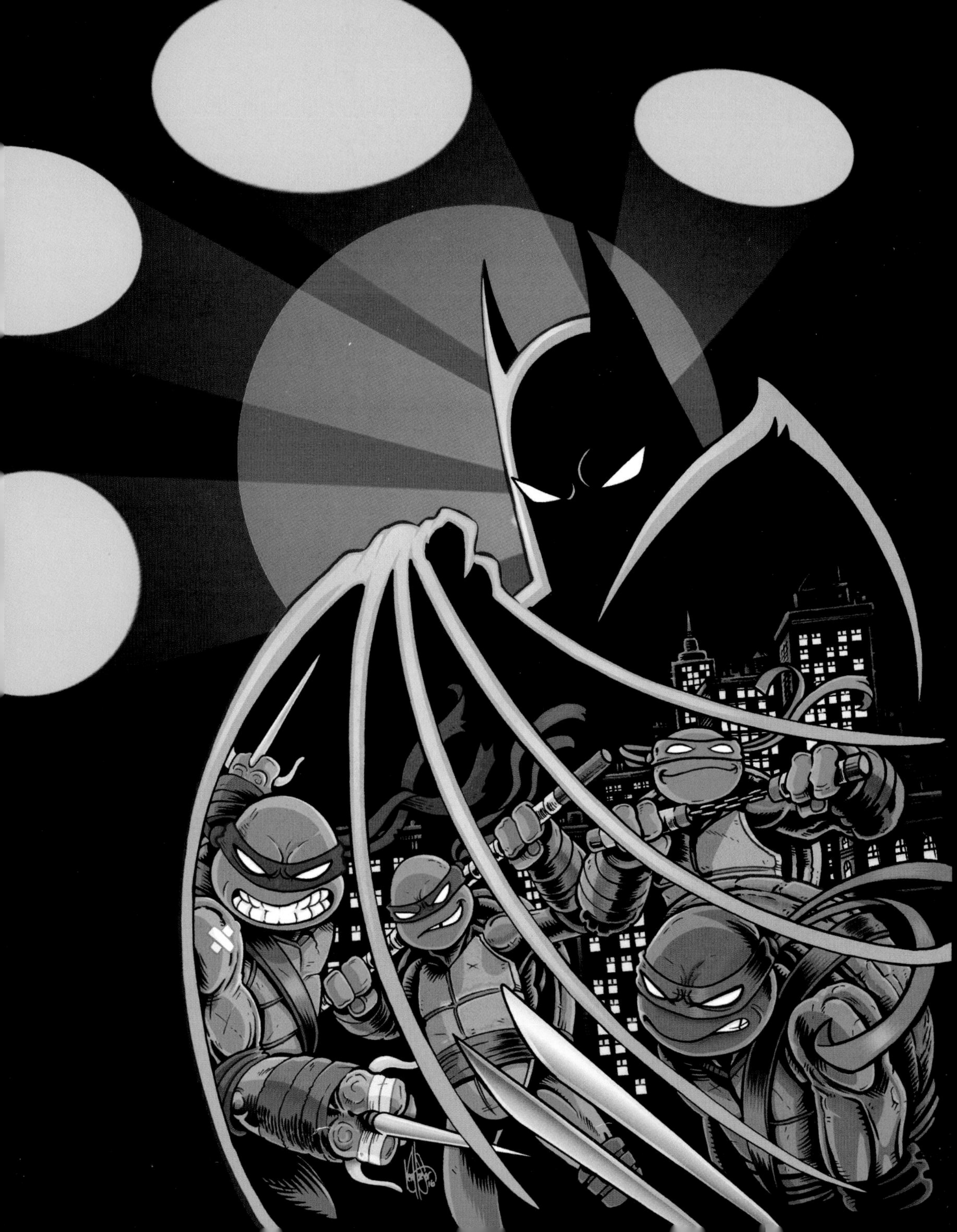

Batman / Teenage Mutant Ninja Turtles Advetnures
is published by Stone Arch Books,
A Capstone Imprint
1710 Roe Crest Drive
North Mankato, Minnesota 56003
www.mycapstonepub.com

Originally published as BATMAN/TEENAGE MUTANT NINJA TURTLES ADVENTURES issue #1.

Special thanks to Jim Chadwick, Joan Hilty, Linda Lee, and Kat van Dam for their invaluable assistance.

Cataloging-in-Publication Data is available at the Library of Congress website:
ISBN 978-1-4965-7381-0 (library binding)
ISBN 978-1-4965-7389-6 (eBook PDF)

Summary: While Batman investigates Two-Face's mysterious escape from Arkham Prison, the Teenage Mutant Ninja Turtles battle Clayface.

STONE ARCH BOOKS
Donald Lemke Editorial Director
Gena Chester Editor
Hilary Wacholz Art Director
Kathy McColley Production Specialist

Batman created by Bob Kane with Bill Finger

BATMAN TEENAGE MUTANT NINJA TURTLES ADVENTURES

THE FACE OF TWO WORLDS

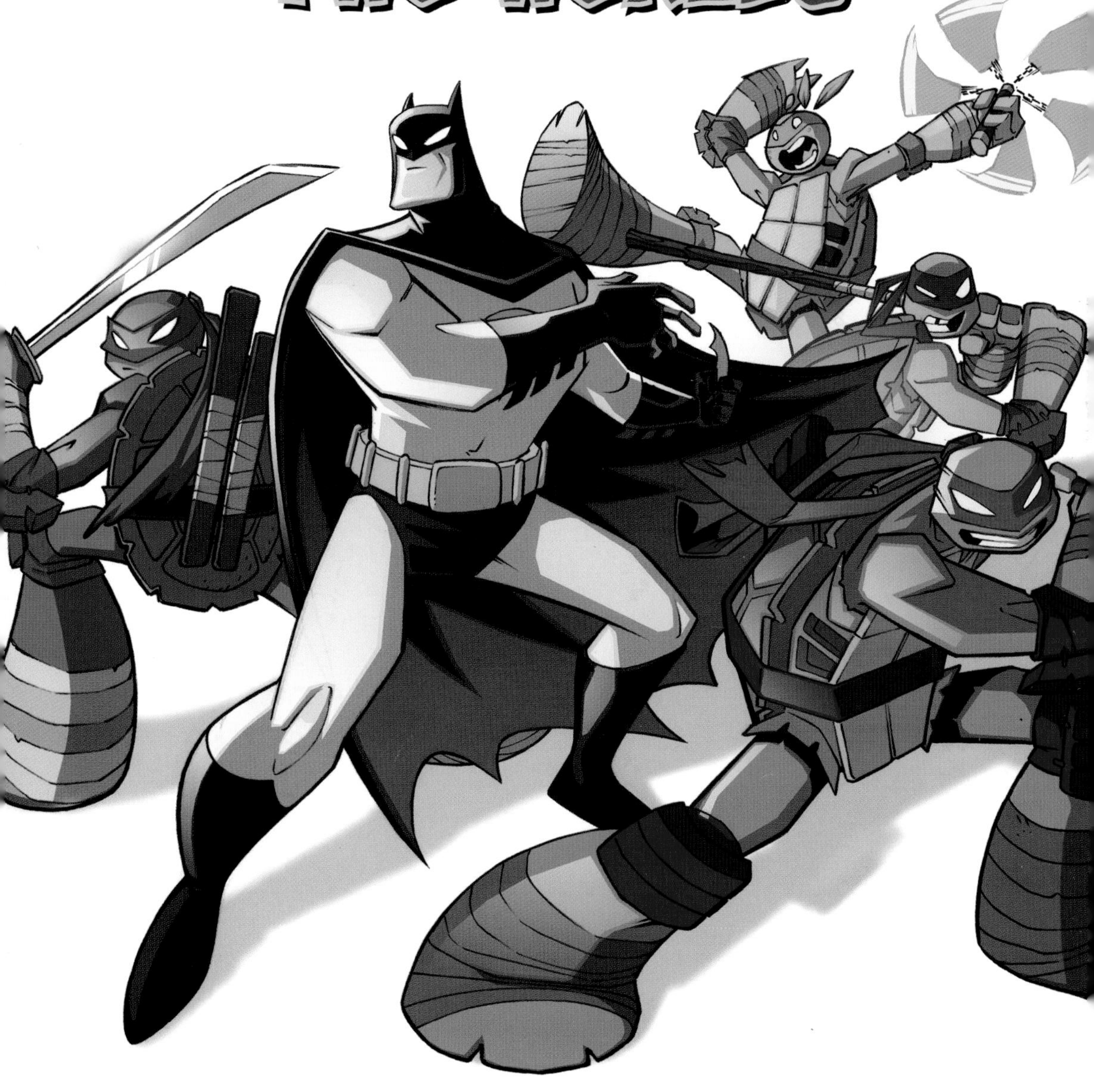

WRITER: MATTHEW K. MANNING | ARTIST: JON SOMMARIVA
INKER: SEAN PARSONS | COLORIST: LEONARDO ITO

STONE ARCH BOOKS
a capstone imprint

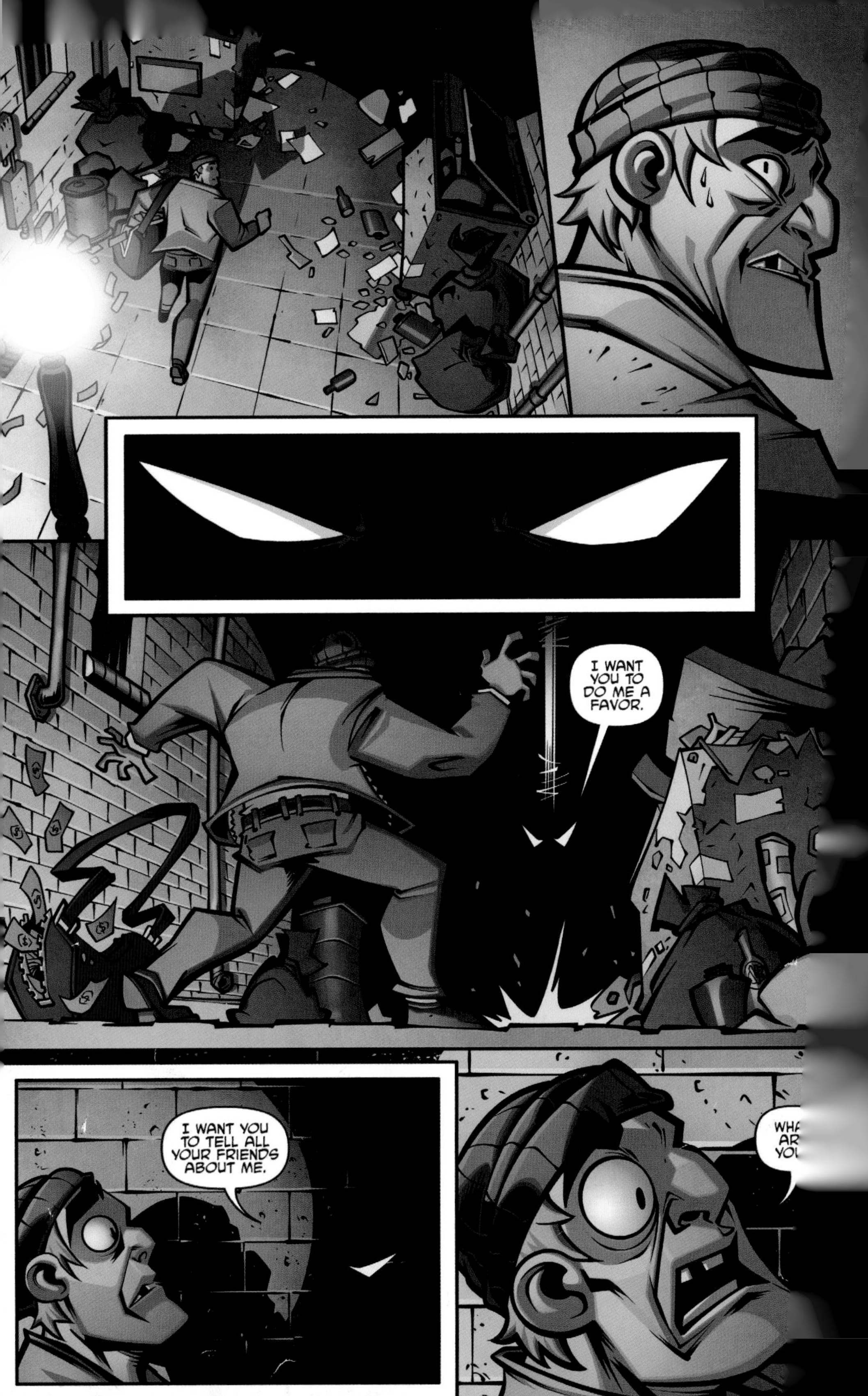
I WANT YOU TO DO ME A FAVOR.
I WANT YOU TO TELL ALL YOUR FRIENDS ABOUT ME.

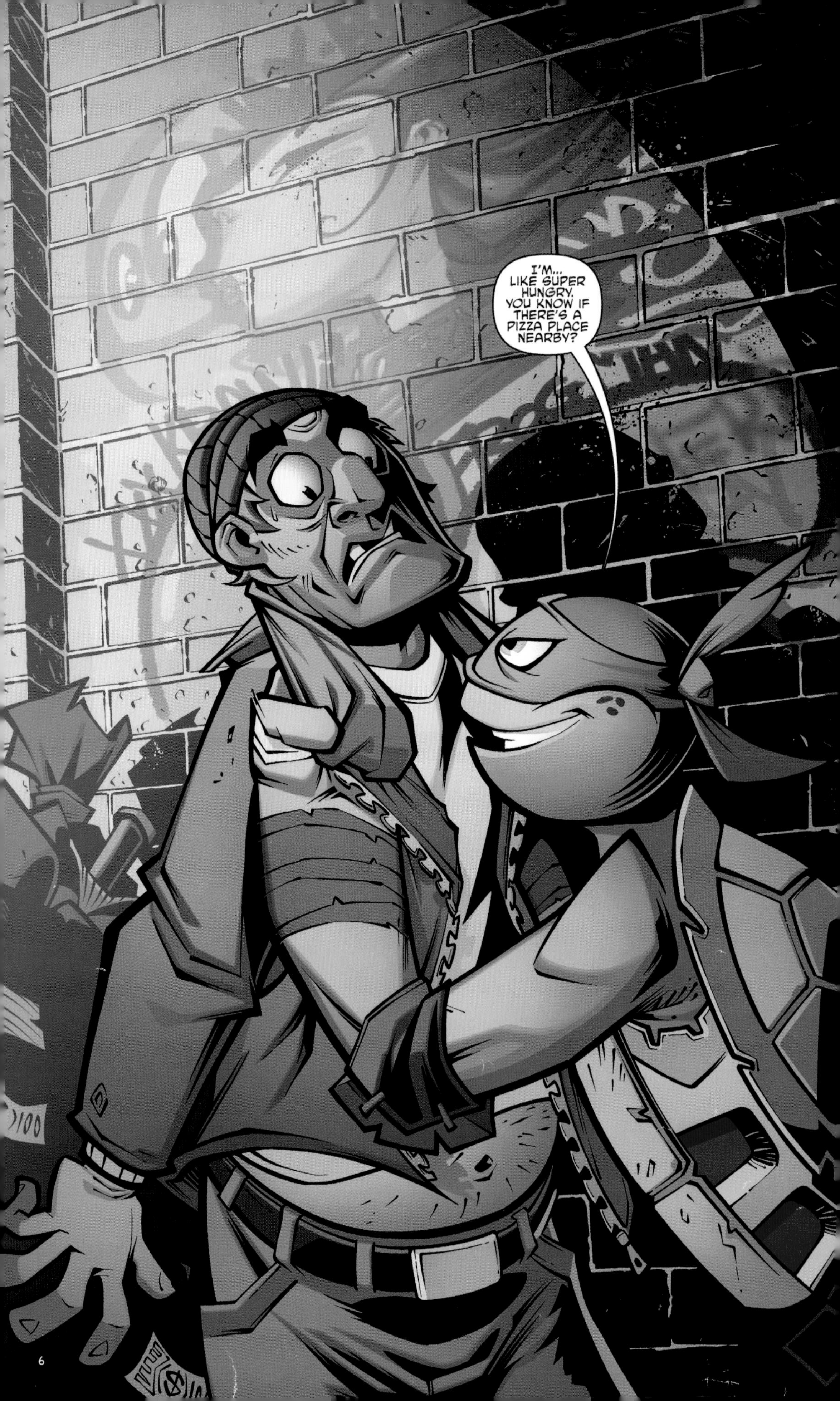
I'M... LIKE SUPER HUNGRY. YOU KNOW IF THERE'S A PIZZA PLACE NEARBY?

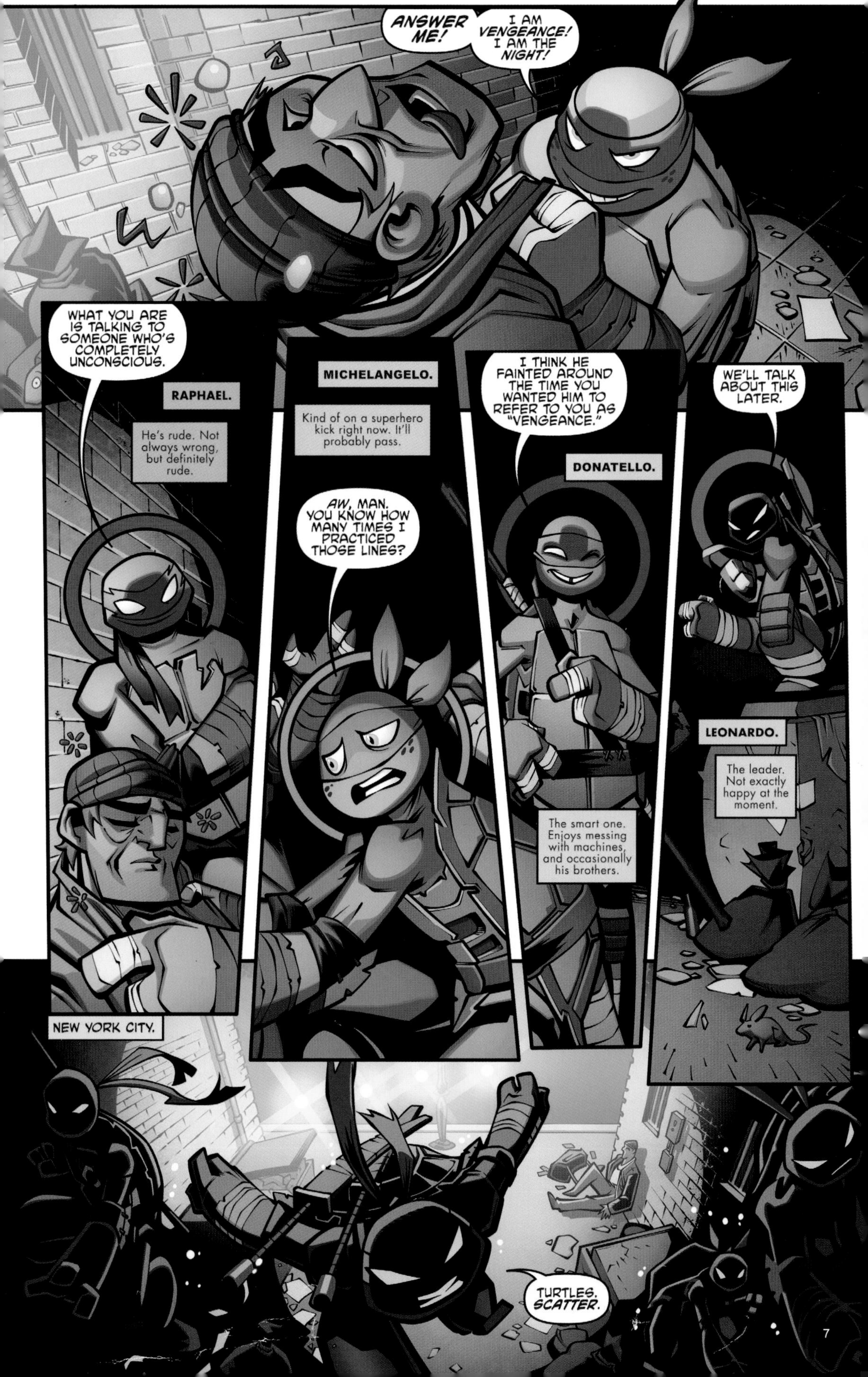

ANSWER ME!
I AM VENGEANCE! I AM THE NIGHT!
WHAT YOU ARE IS TALKING TO SOMEONE WHO'S COMPLETELY UNCONSCIOUS.
RAPHAEL.
He's rude. Not always wrong, but definitely rude.
MICHELANGELO.
Kind of on a superhero kick right now. It'll probably pass.
AW, MAN. YOU KNOW HOW MANY TIMES I PRACTICED THOSE LINES?
I THINK HE FAINTED AROUND THE TIME YOU WANTED HIM TO REFER TO YOU AS "VENGEANCE."
DONATELLO.
The smart one. Enjoys messing with machines, and occasionally his brothers.
WE'LL TALK ABOUT THIS LATER.
LEONARDO.
The leader. Not exactly happy at the moment.
NEW YORK CITY.
TURTLES. SCATTER.

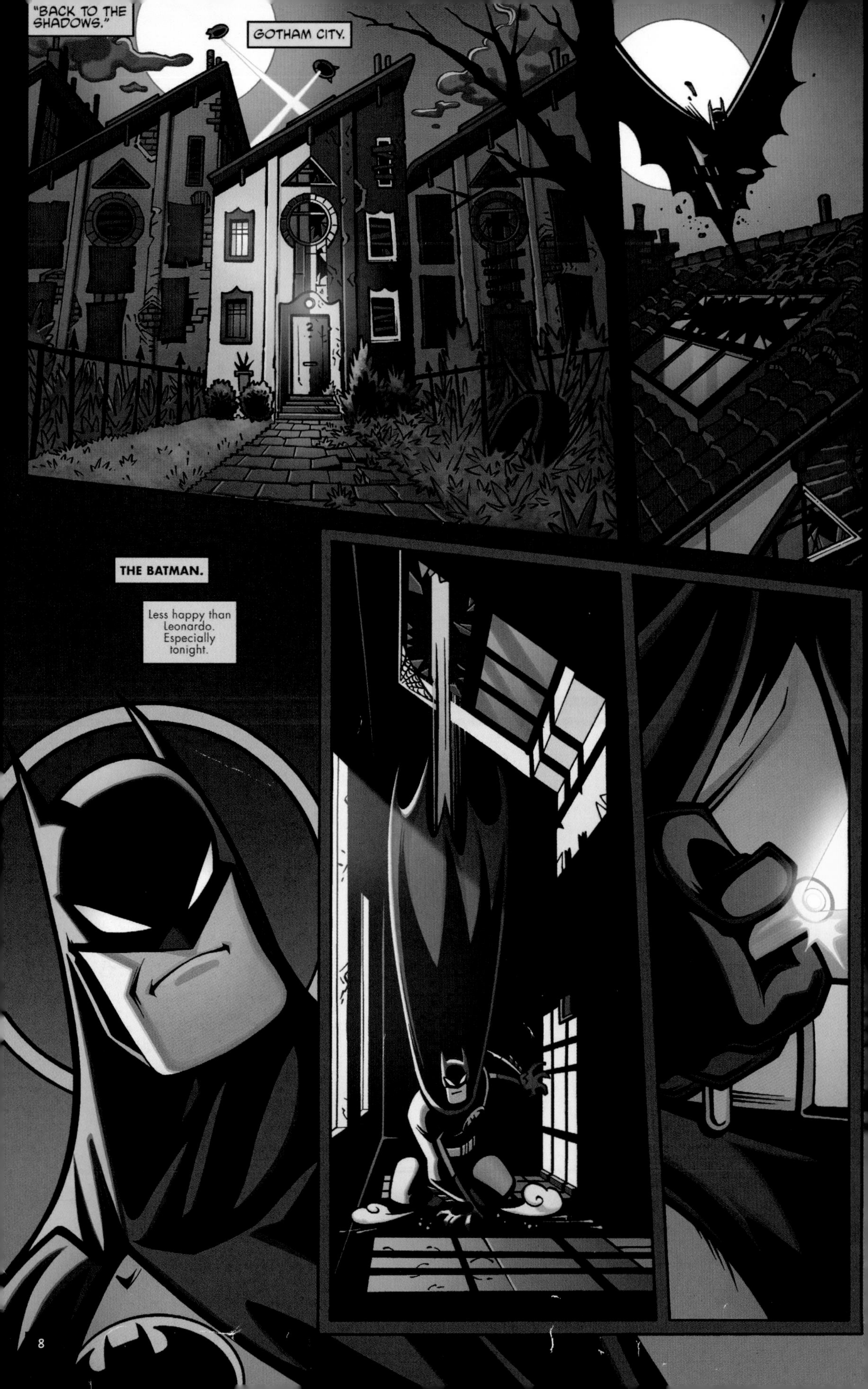
"BACK TO THE SHADOWS."
GOTHAM CITY.
THE BATMAN.
Less happy than Leonardo. Especially tonight.

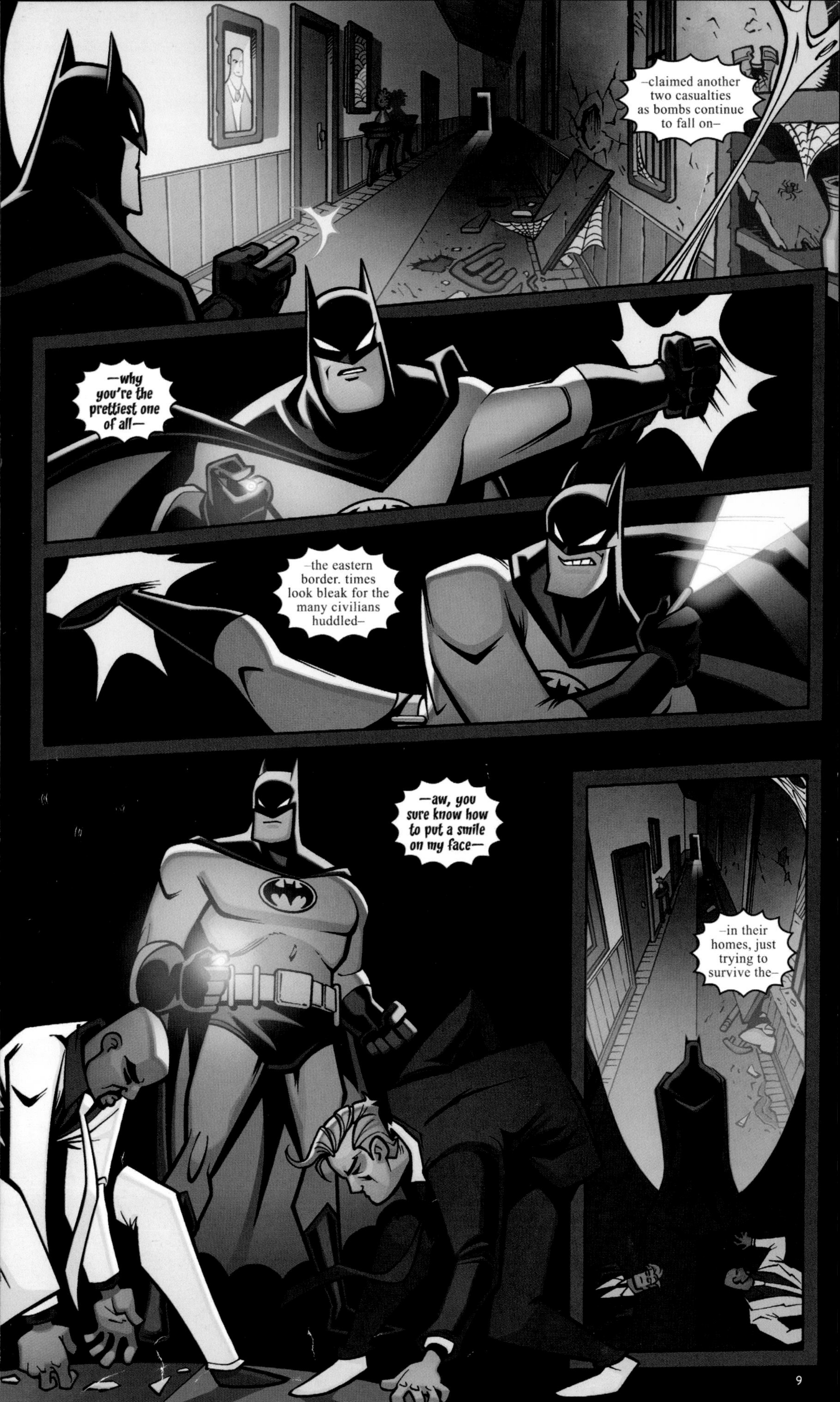

–claimed another two casualties as bombs continue to fall on–
—why you're the prettiest one of all—
–the eastern border. times look bleak for the many civilians huddled–
—aw, you sure know how to put a smile on my face—
–in their homes, just trying to survive the–

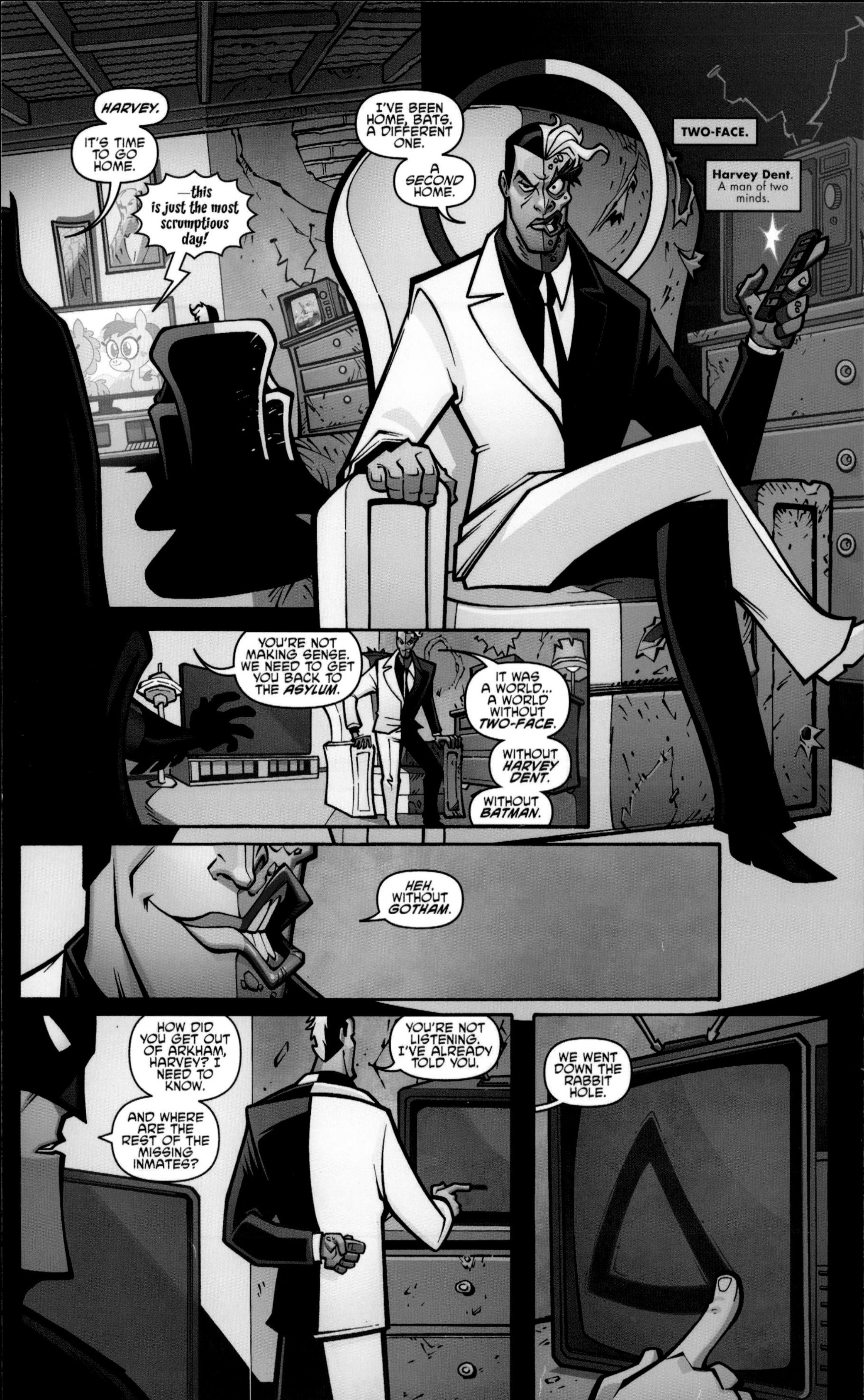
HARVEY.
IT'S TIME TO GO HOME.
—this is just the most scrumptious day!
I'VE BEEN HOME, BATS. A DIFFERENT ONE.
A SECOND HOME.
TWO-FACE.
Harvey Dent. A man of two minds.
YOU'RE NOT MAKING SENSE. WE NEED TO GET YOU BACK TO THE ASYLUM.
IT WAS A WORLD... A WORLD WITHOUT TWO-FACE.
WITHOUT HARVEY DENT.
WITHOUT BATMAN.
HEH. WITHOUT GOTHAM.
HOW DID YOU GET OUT OF ARKHAM, HARVEY? I NEED TO KNOW.
AND WHERE ARE THE REST OF THE MISSING INMATES?
YOU'RE NOT LISTENING. I'VE ALREADY TOLD YOU.
WE WENT DOWN THE RABBIT HOLE.

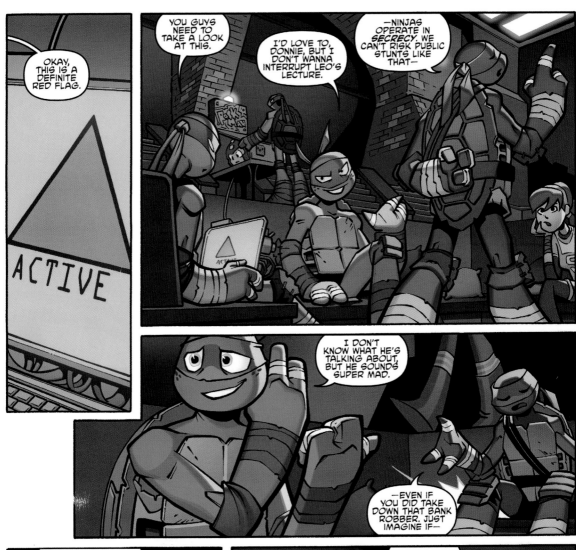

OKAY, THIS IS A DEFINITE RED FLAG.

ACTIVE

YOU GUYS NEED TO TAKE A LOOK AT THIS.

I'D LOVE TO, DONNIE, BUT I DON'T WANNA INTERRUPT LEO'S LECTURE.

—NINJAS OPERATE IN *SECRECY*. WE CAN'T RISK PUBLIC STUNTS LIKE THAT—

I DON'T KNOW WHAT HE'S TALKING ABOUT, BUT HE SOUNDS SUPER MAD.

—EVEN IF YOU DID TAKE DOWN THAT BANK ROBBER. JUST IMAGINE IF—

GUYS, I HATE TO BE THE VOICE OF REASON YET AGAIN, BUT YOU NEED TO STOP THE SQUABBLING AND CHECK THIS OUT.

LIKE, NOW.

APRIL O'NEIL.

The voice of reason. Like she said. Pay attention, already!

IS THAT WHAT I THINK IT IS? THEY'RE BACK?

YEAH. I THINK SO. THERE'S DEFINITELY BEEN PORTAL USE.

AND IT'S STILL ACTIVE.

IT'S *THE KRAANG.*

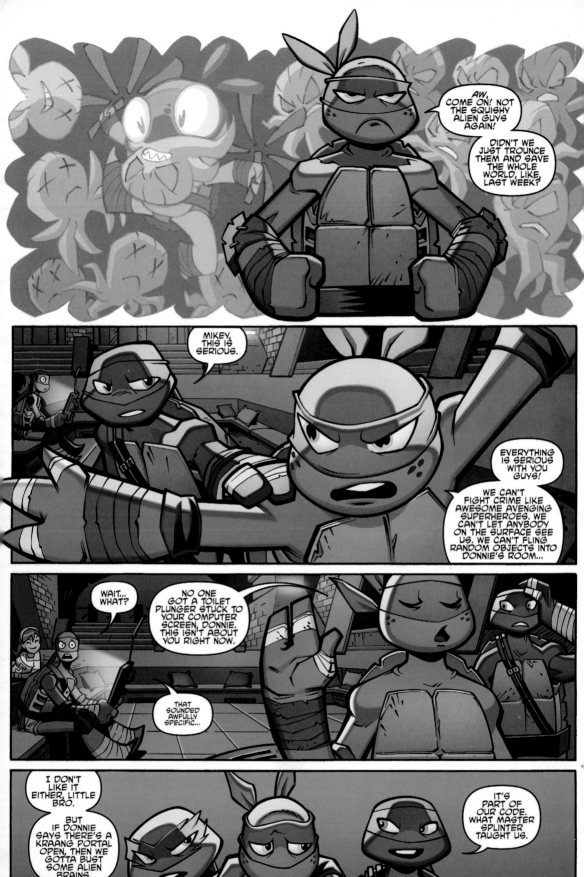

AW, COME ON! NOT THE SQUISHY ALIEN GUYS AGAIN!

DIDN'T WE JUST TROUNCE THEM AND SAVE THE WHOLE WORLD, LIKE, LAST WEEK?

MIKEY, THIS IS SERIOUS.

EVERYTHING IS SERIOUS WITH YOU GUYS!

WE CAN'T FIGHT CRIME LIKE AWESOME AVENGING SUPERHEROES. WE CAN'T LET ANYBODY ON THE SURFACE SEE US. WE CAN'T FLING RANDOM OBJECTS INTO DONNIE'S ROOM...

WAIT... WHAT?

NO ONE GOT A TOILET PLUNGER STUCK TO YOUR COMPUTER SCREEN, DONNIE. THIS ISN'T ABOUT YOU RIGHT NOW.

THAT SOUNDED AWFULLY SPECIFIC...

I DON'T LIKE IT EITHER, LITTLE BRO.

BUT IF DONNIE SAYS THERE'S A KRAANG PORTAL OPEN, THEN WE GOTTA BUST SOME ALIEN BRAINS.

IT'S PART OF OUR CODE. WHAT MASTER SPLINTER TAUGHT US.

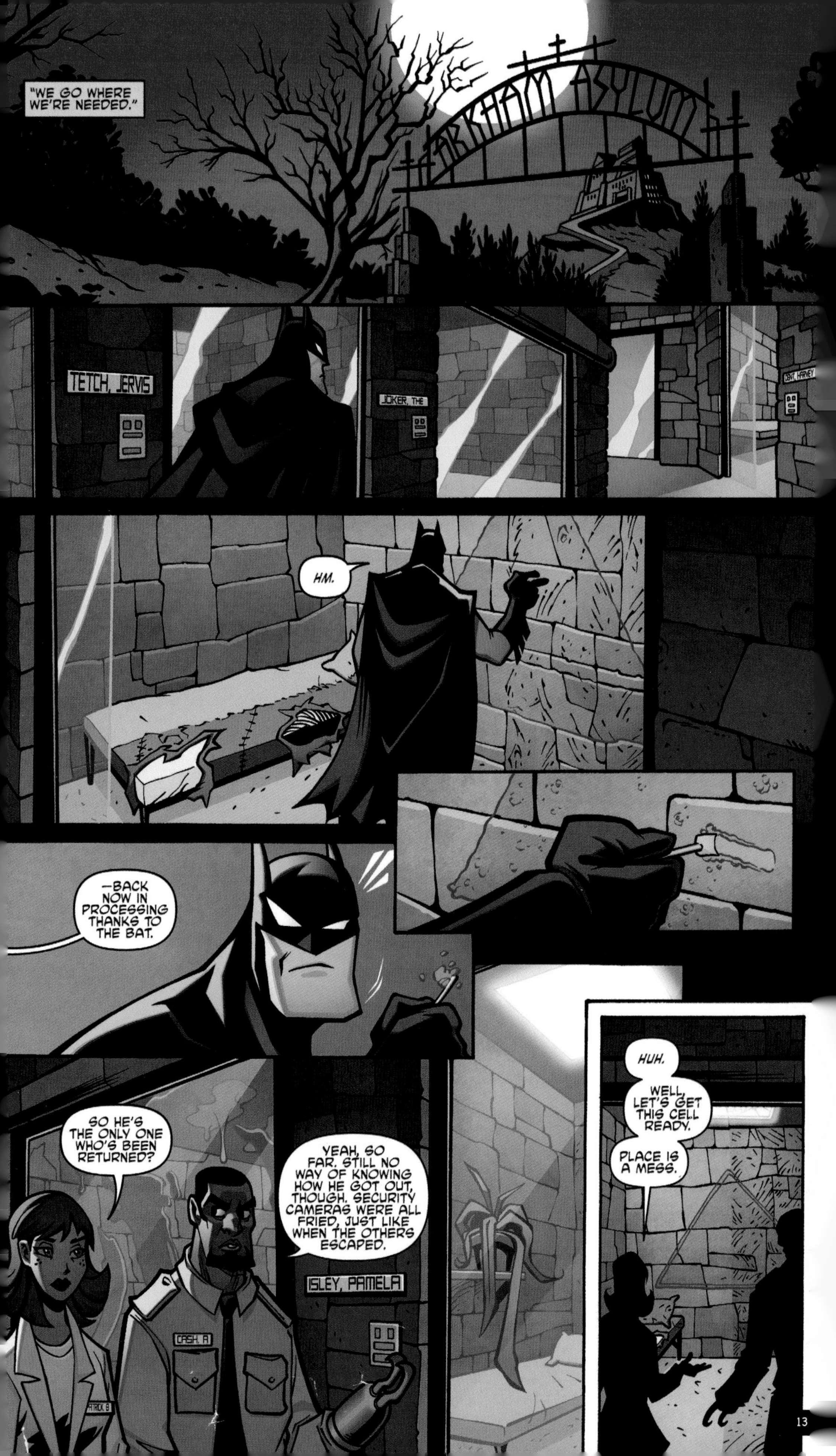

"WE GO WHERE WE'RE NEEDED."
ARKHAM ASYLUM
TETCH, JERVIS
JOKER, THE
HM.
—BACK NOW IN PROCESSING THANKS TO THE BAT.
SO HE'S THE ONLY ONE WHO'S BEEN RETURNED?
YEAH, SO FAR. STILL NO WAY OF KNOWING HOW HE GOT OUT, THOUGH. SECURITY CAMERAS WERE ALL FRIED, JUST LIKE WHEN THE OTHERS ESCAPED.
ISLEY, PAMELA
CASH, A
HUH.
WELL, LET'S GET THIS CELL READY.
PLACE IS A MESS.

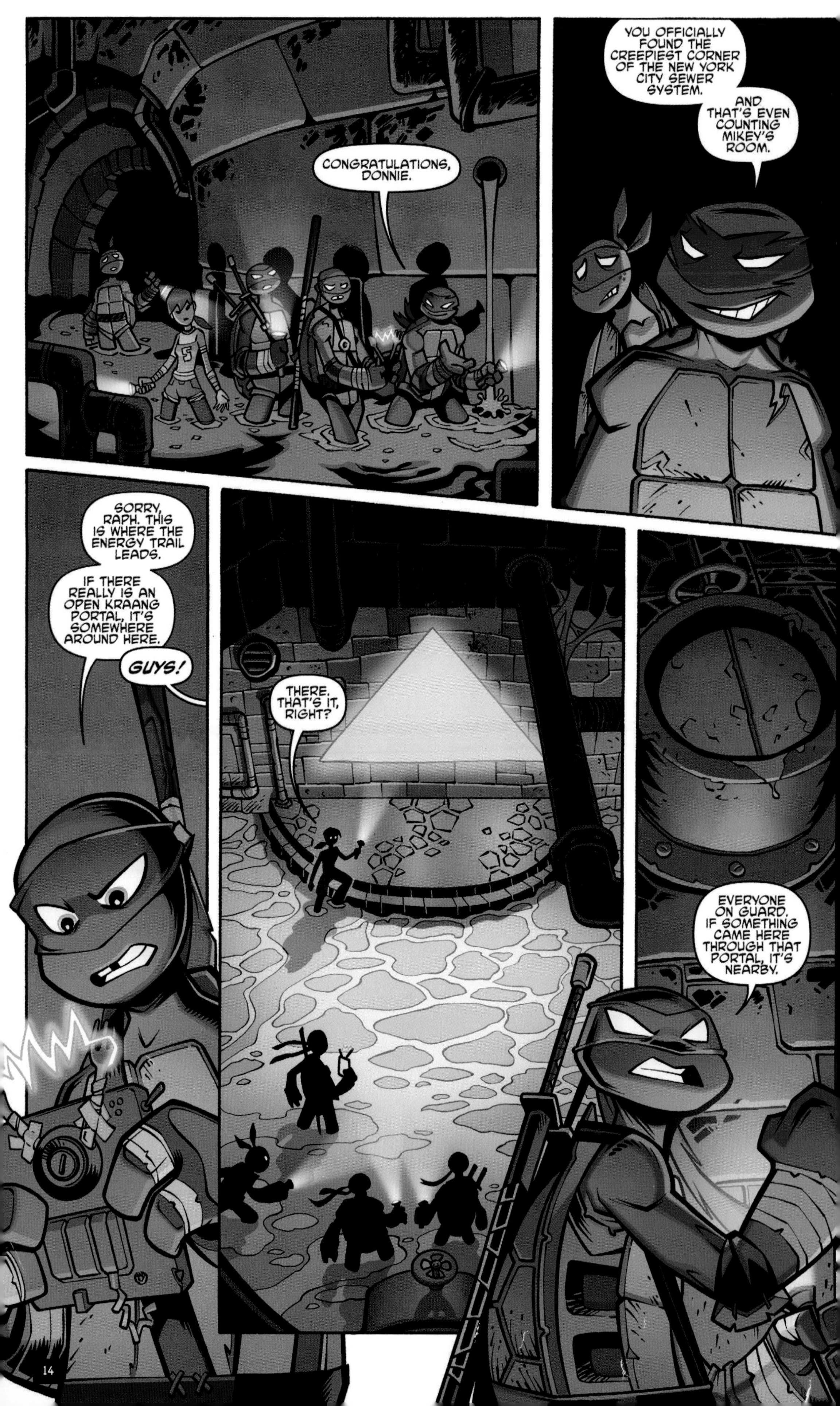
CONGRATULATIONS, DONNIE.
YOU OFFICIALLY FOUND THE CREEPIEST CORNER OF THE NEW YORK CITY SEWER SYSTEM.
AND THAT'S EVEN COUNTING MIKEY'S ROOM.
SORRY, RAPH. THIS IS WHERE THE ENERGY TRAIL LEADS.
IF THERE REALLY IS AN OPEN KRAANG PORTAL, IT'S SOMEWHERE AROUND HERE.
GUYS!
THERE. THAT'S IT, RIGHT?
EVERYONE ON GUARD. IF SOMETHING CAME HERE THROUGH THAT PORTAL, IT'S NEARBY.

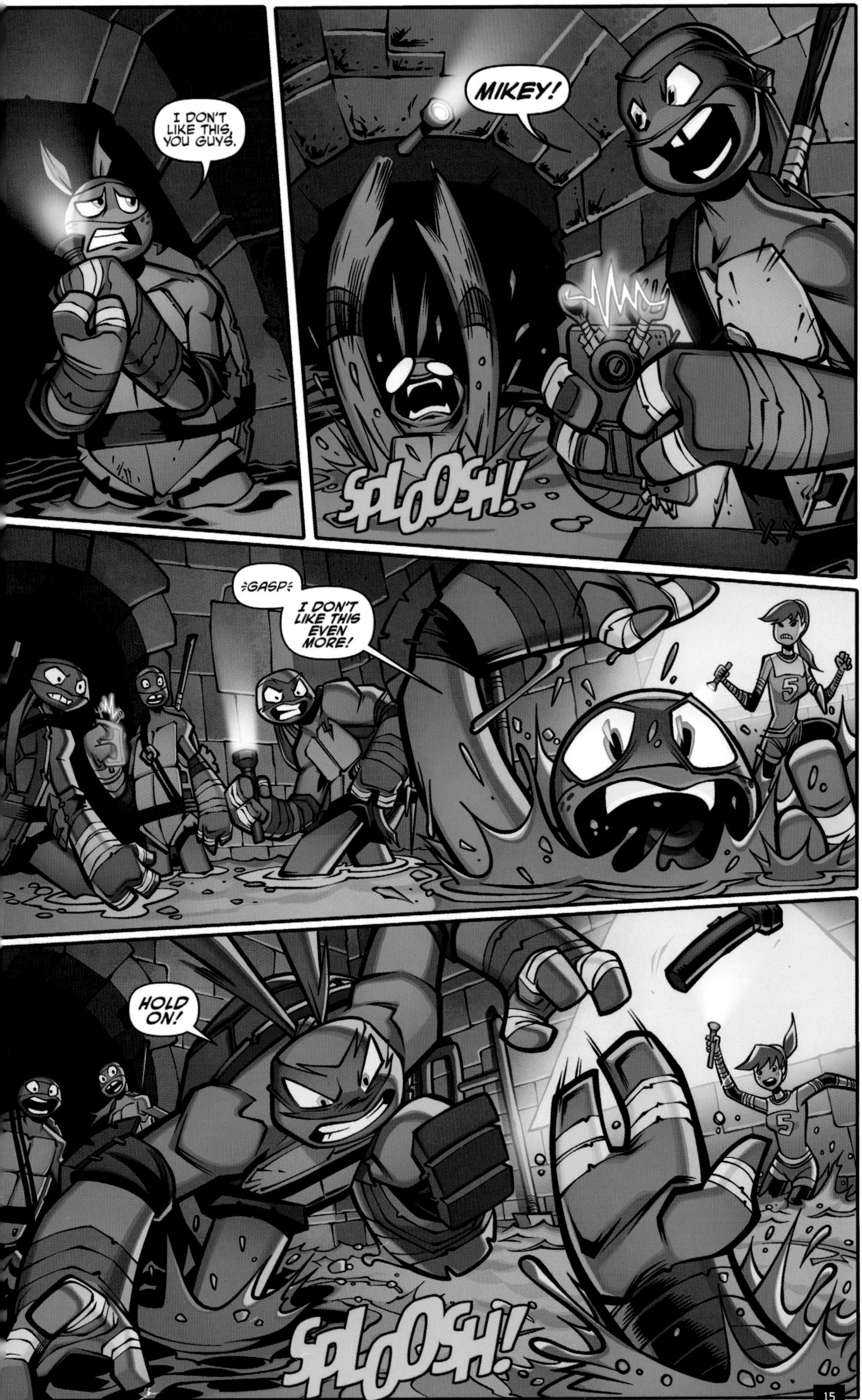
I DON'T LIKE THIS, YOU GUYS.
MIKEY!
SPLOOSH!
≑GASP≑
I DON'T LIKE THIS EVEN MORE!
HOLD ON!
5
5
SPLOOSH!

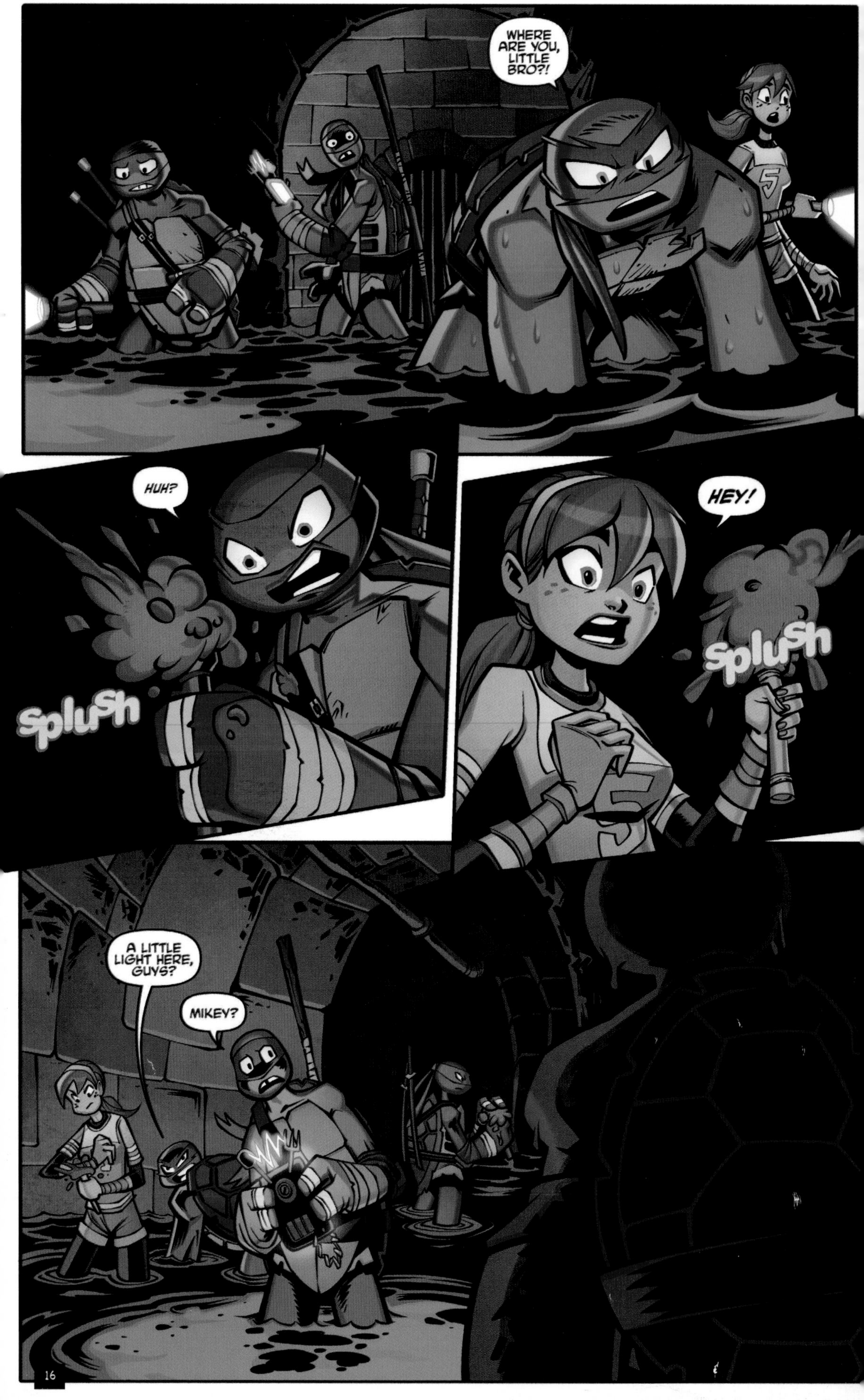
WHERE ARE YOU, LITTLE BRO?!
HUH?
SPLUSH
HEY!
SPLUSH
A LITTLE LIGHT HERE, GUYS?
MIKEY?

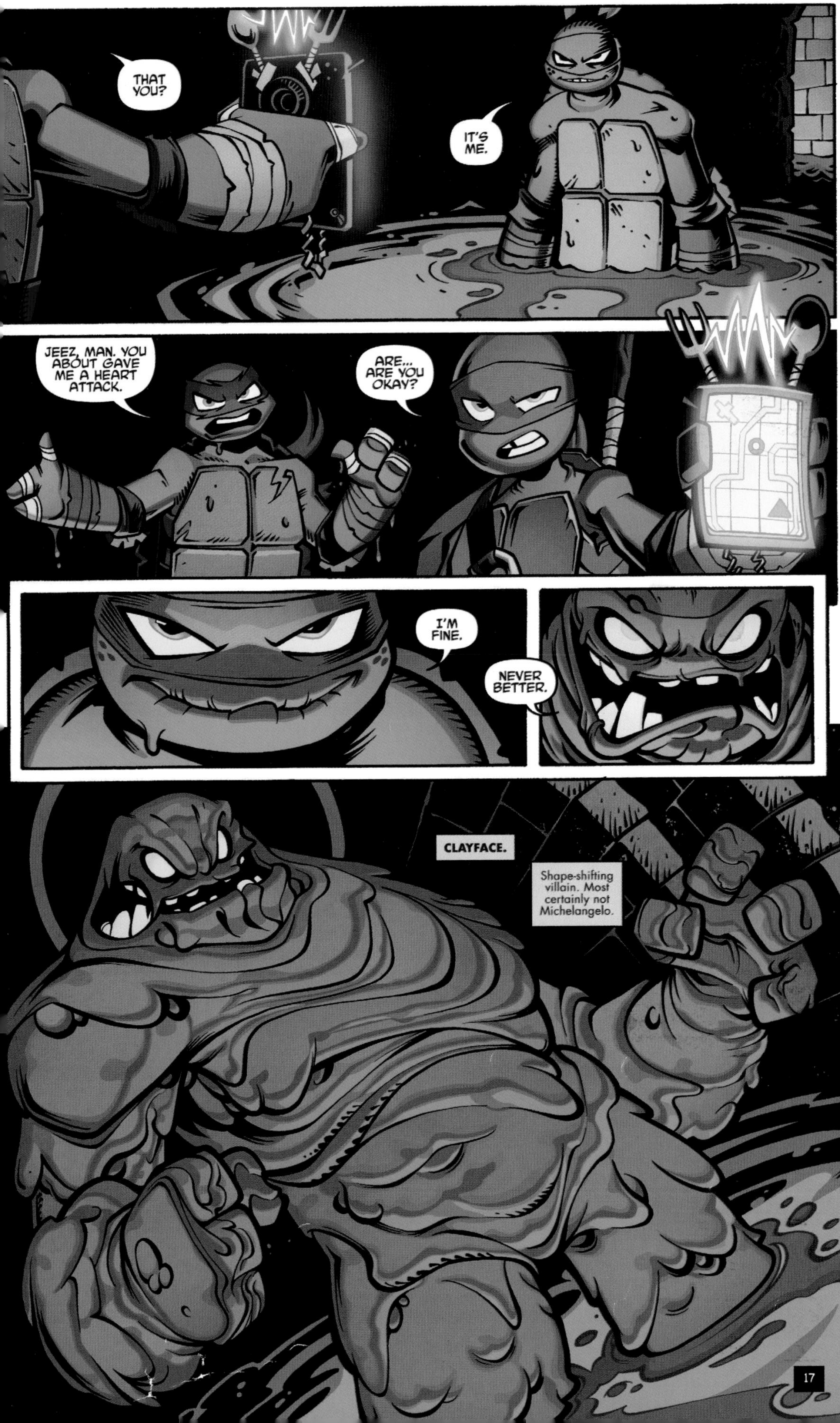
THAT YOU?
IT'S ME.
JEEZ, MAN. YOU ABOUT GAVE ME A HEART ATTACK.
ARE... ARE YOU OKAY?
I'M FINE.
NEVER BETTER.
CLAYFACE.
Shape-shifting villain. Most certainly not Michelangelo.

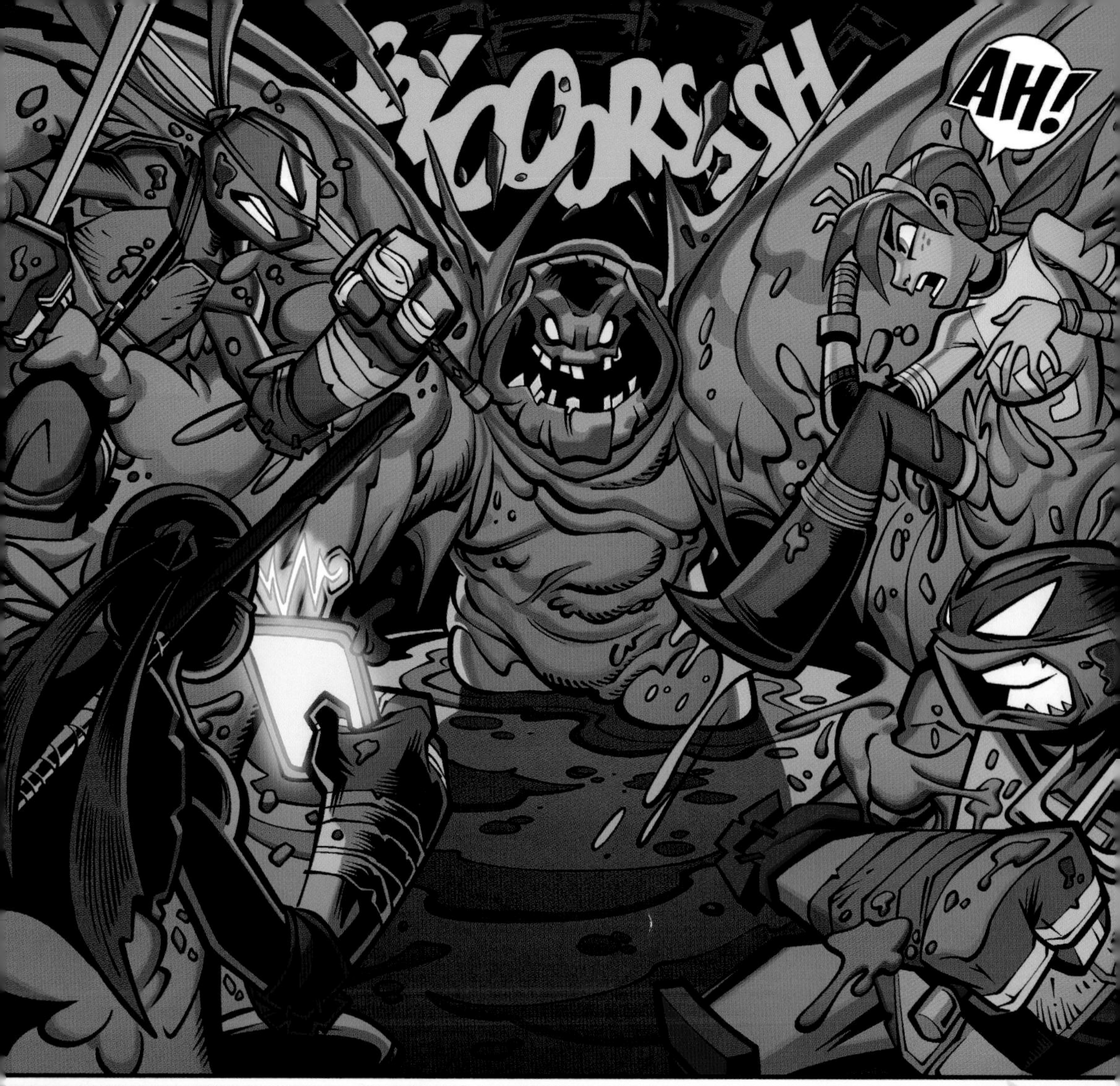
KKOOORSSSH
AH!

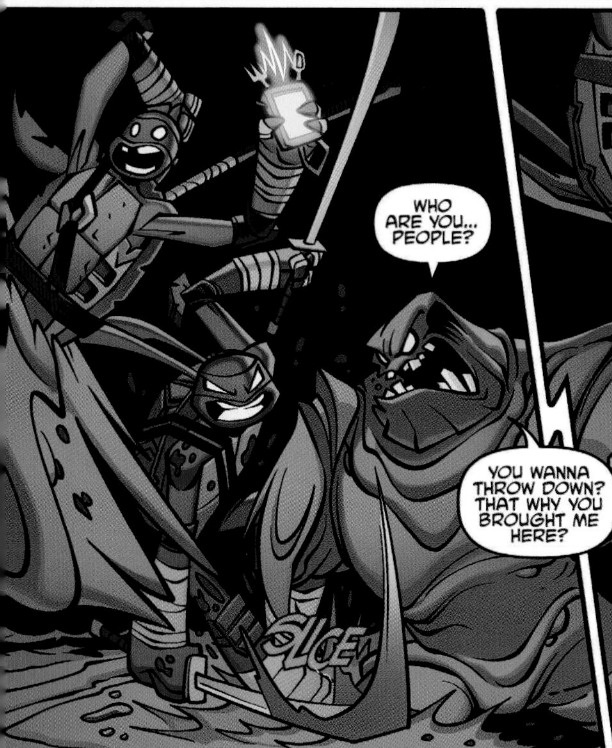
WHO ARE YOU... PEOPLE?
YOU WANNA THROW DOWN? THAT WHY YOU BROUGHT ME HERE?
SLICE

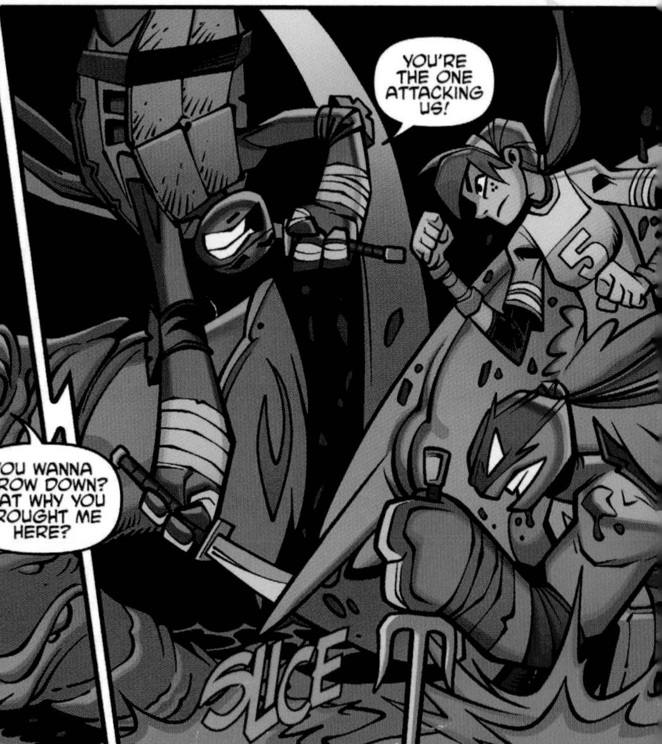
YOU'RE THE ONE ATTACKING US!
SLICE

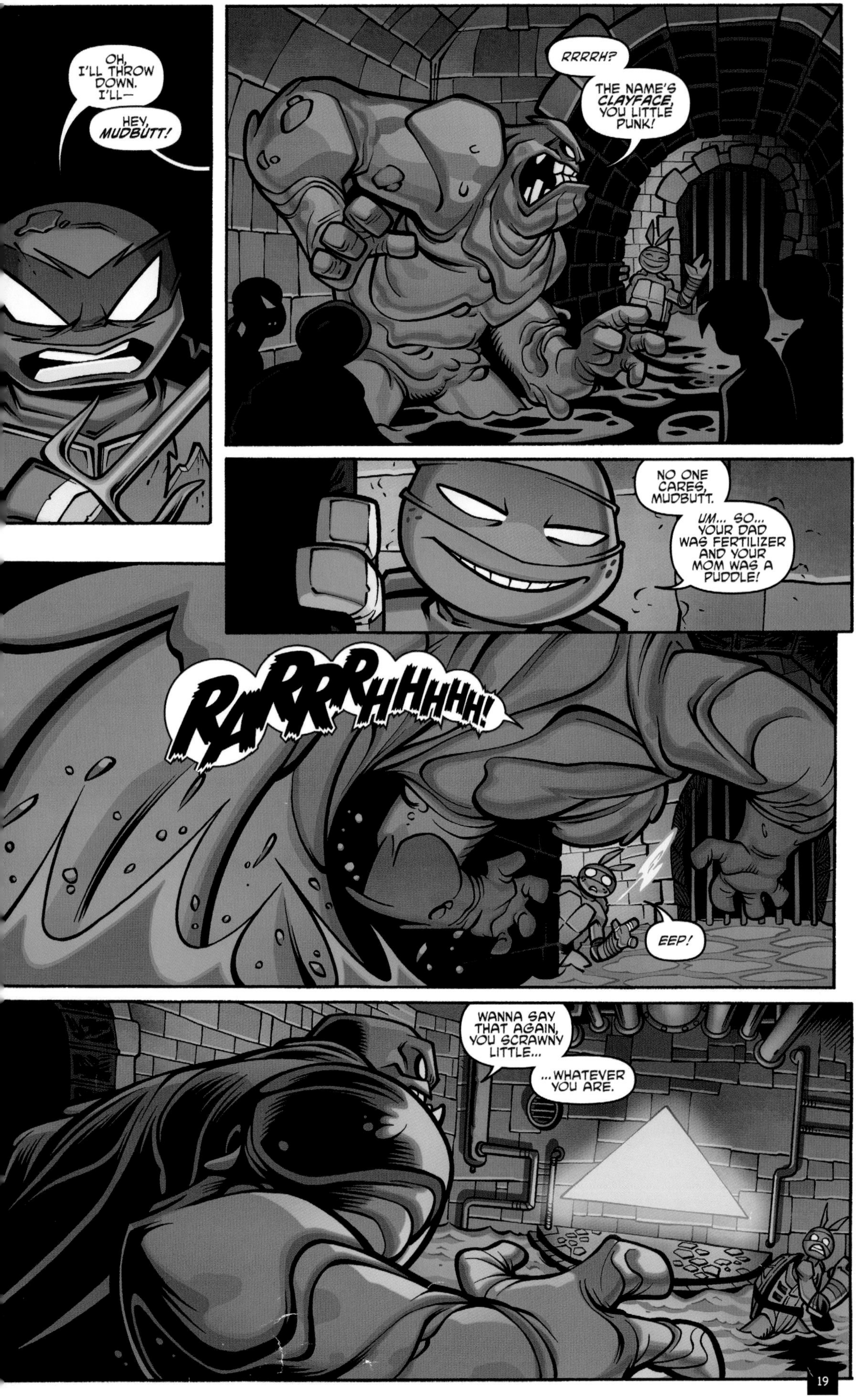
OH, I'LL THROW DOWN. I'LL—
HEY, MUDBUTT!
RRRRH?
THE NAME'S CLAYFACE, YOU LITTLE PUNK!
NO ONE CARES, MUDBUTT.
UM... SO... YOUR DAD WAS FERTILIZER AND YOUR MOM WAS A PUDDLE!
RARRRHHHHH!
EEP!
WANNA SAY THAT AGAIN, YOU SCRAWNY LITTLE...
...WHATEVER YOU ARE.

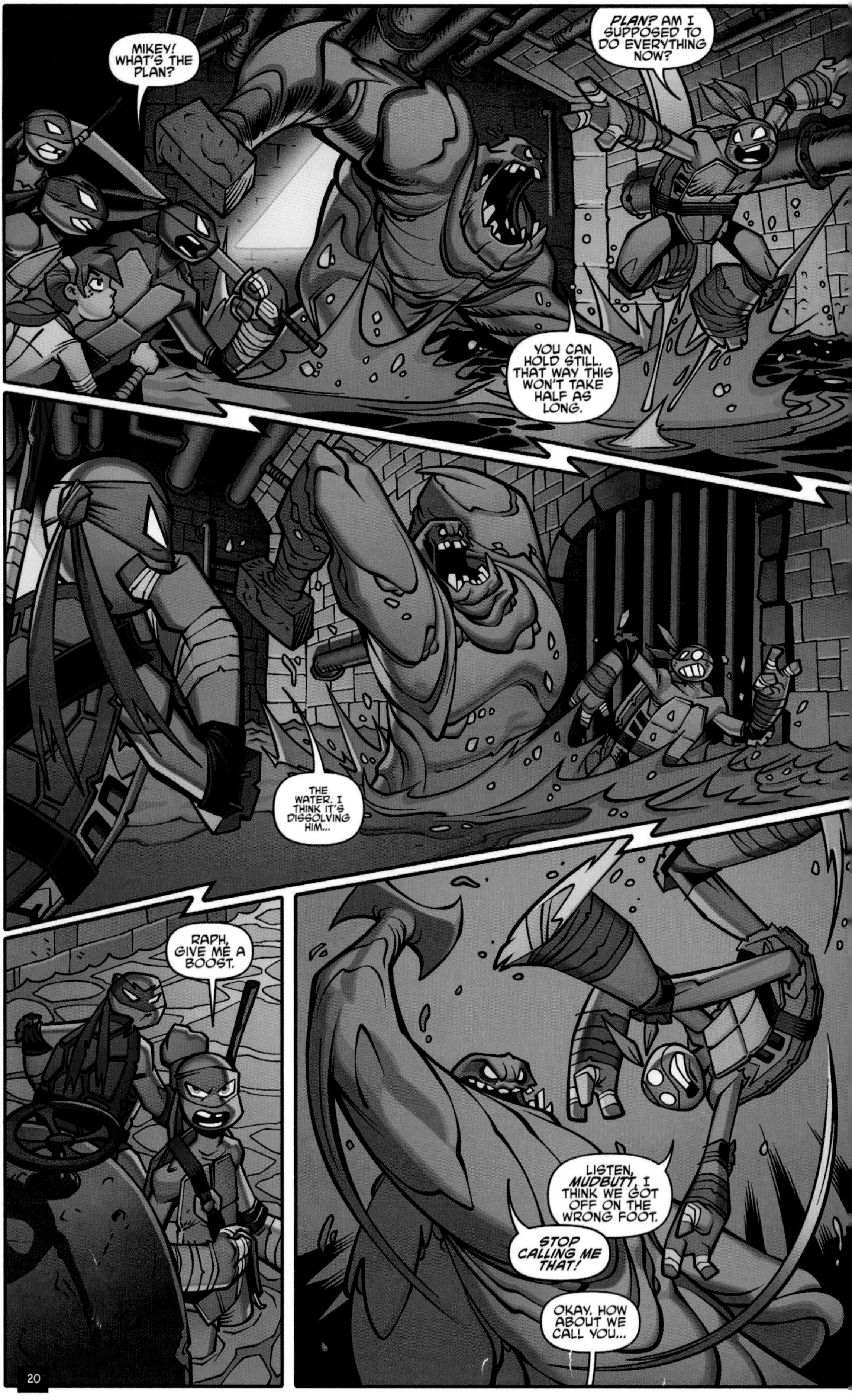

MIKEY! WHAT'S THE PLAN?
PLAN? AM I SUPPOSED TO DO EVERYTHING NOW?
YOU CAN HOLD STILL. THAT WAY THIS WON'T TAKE HALF AS LONG.
THE WATER. I THINK IT'S DISSOLVING HIM...
RAPH, GIVE ME A BOOST.
LISTEN, MUDBUTT, I THINK WE GOT OFF ON THE WRONG FOOT.
STOP CALLING ME THAT!
OKAY. HOW ABOUT WE CALL YOU...

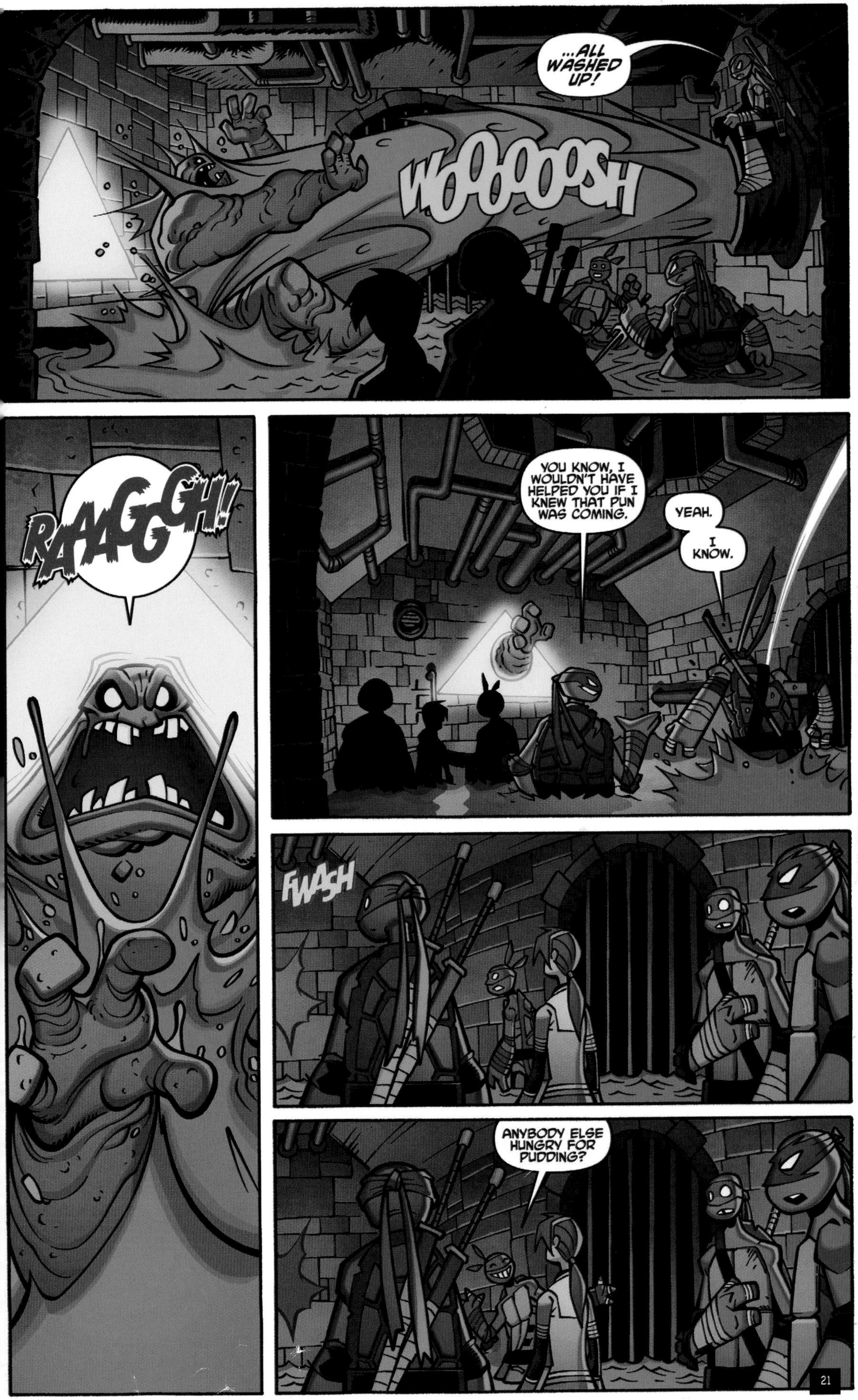
...ALL WASHED UP!
WOOOOOSH
RAAGGGH!
YOU KNOW, I WOULDN'T HAVE HELPED YOU IF I KNEW THAT PUN WAS COMING.
YEAH.
I KNOW.
FWASH
ANYBODY ELSE HUNGRY FOR PUDDING?

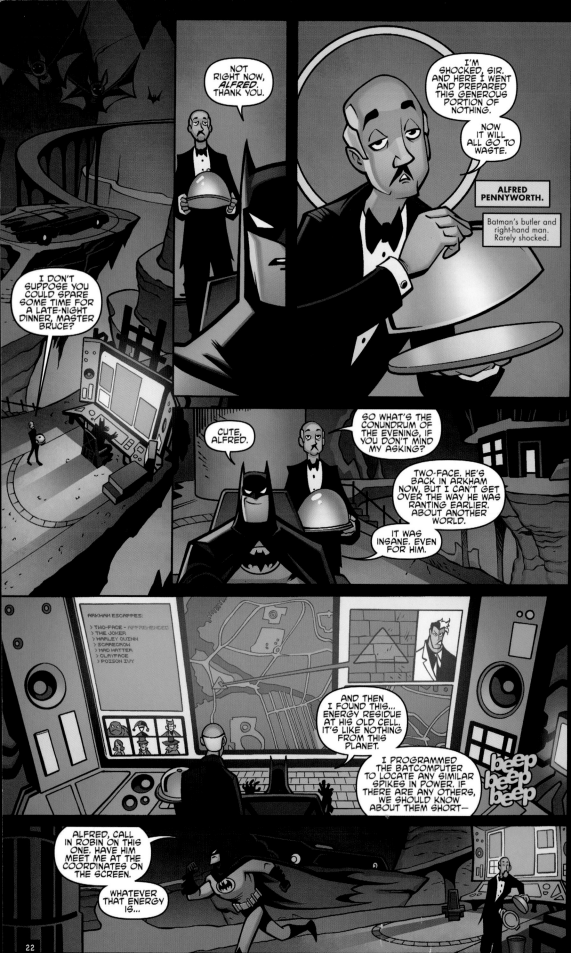

NOT RIGHT NOW, *ALFRED.* THANK YOU.

I'M SHOCKED, SIR. AND HERE I WENT AND PREPARED THIS GENEROUS PORTION OF NOTHING.

NOW IT WILL ALL GO TO WASTE.

ALFRED PENNYWORTH.

Batman's butler and right-hand man. Rarely shocked.

I DON'T SUPPOSE YOU COULD SPARE SOME TIME FOR A LATE-NIGHT DINNER, MASTER BRUCE?

CUTE, ALFRED.

SO WHAT'S THE CONUNDRUM OF THE EVENING, IF YOU DON'T MIND MY ASKING?

TWO-FACE. HE'S BACK IN ARKHAM NOW, BUT I CAN'T GET OVER THE WAY HE WAS RANTING EARLIER. ABOUT ANOTHER WORLD.

IT WAS INSANE. EVEN FOR HIM.

ARKHAM ESCAPEES:

> TWO-FACE - APPREHENDED
> THE JOKER
> HARLEY QUINN
> SCARECROW
> MAD HATTER
> CLAYFACE
> POISON IVY

AND THEN I FOUND THIS... ENERGY RESIDUE AT HIS OLD CELL. IT'S LIKE NOTHING FROM THIS PLANET.

I PROGRAMMED THE BATCOMPUTER TO LOCATE ANY SIMILAR SPIKES IN POWER. IF THERE ARE ANY OTHERS, WE SHOULD KNOW ABOUT THEM SHORT—

beep beep beep

ALFRED, CALL IN ROBIN ON THIS ONE. HAVE HIM MEET ME AT THE COORDINATES ON THE SCREEN.

WHATEVER THAT ENERGY IS...

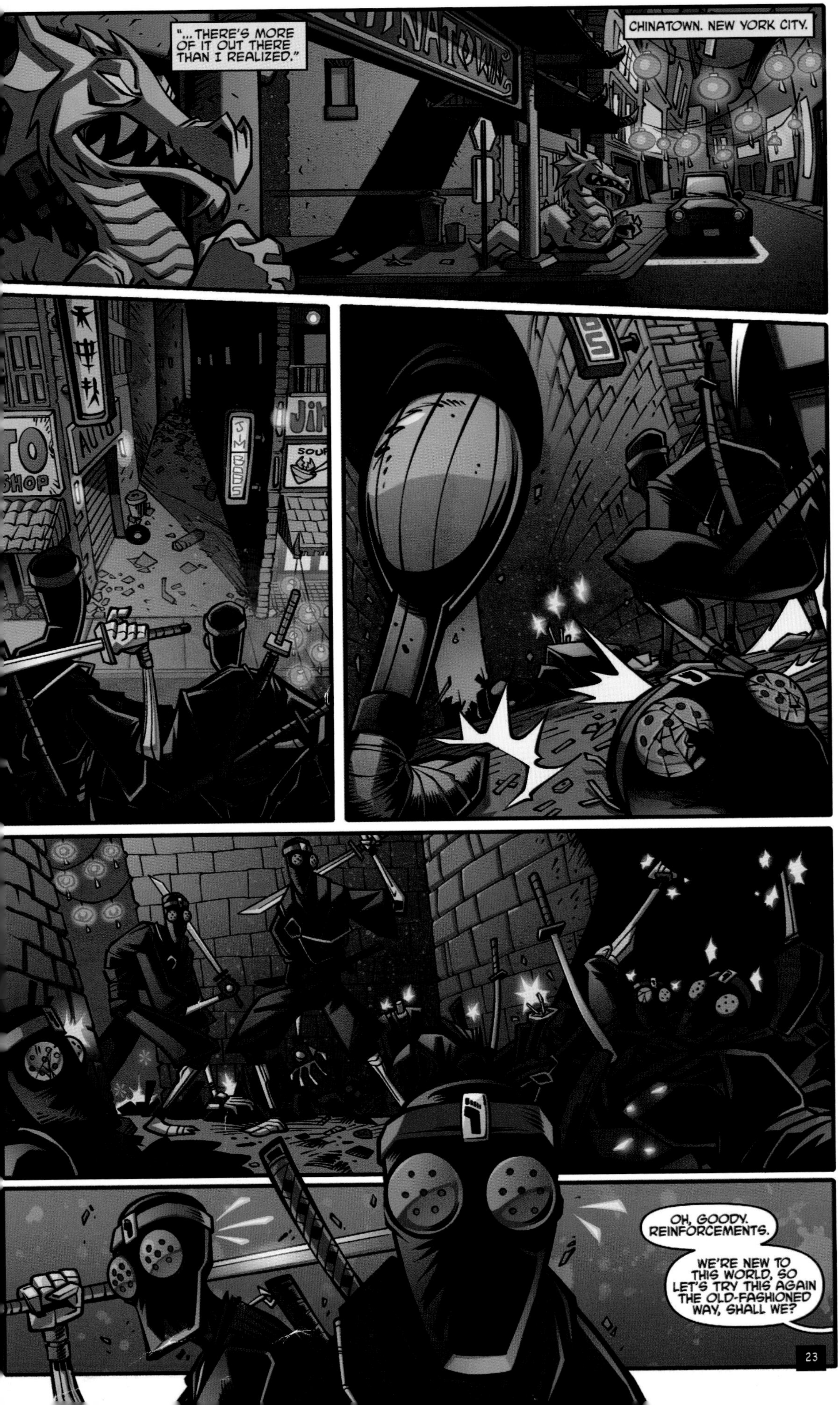
"...THERE'S MORE OF IT OUT THERE THAN I REALIZED."
CHINATOWN. NEW YORK CITY.
OH, GOODY. REINFORCEMENTS.
WE'RE NEW TO THIS WORLD, SO LET'S TRY THIS AGAIN THE OLD-FASHIONED WAY, SHALL WE?

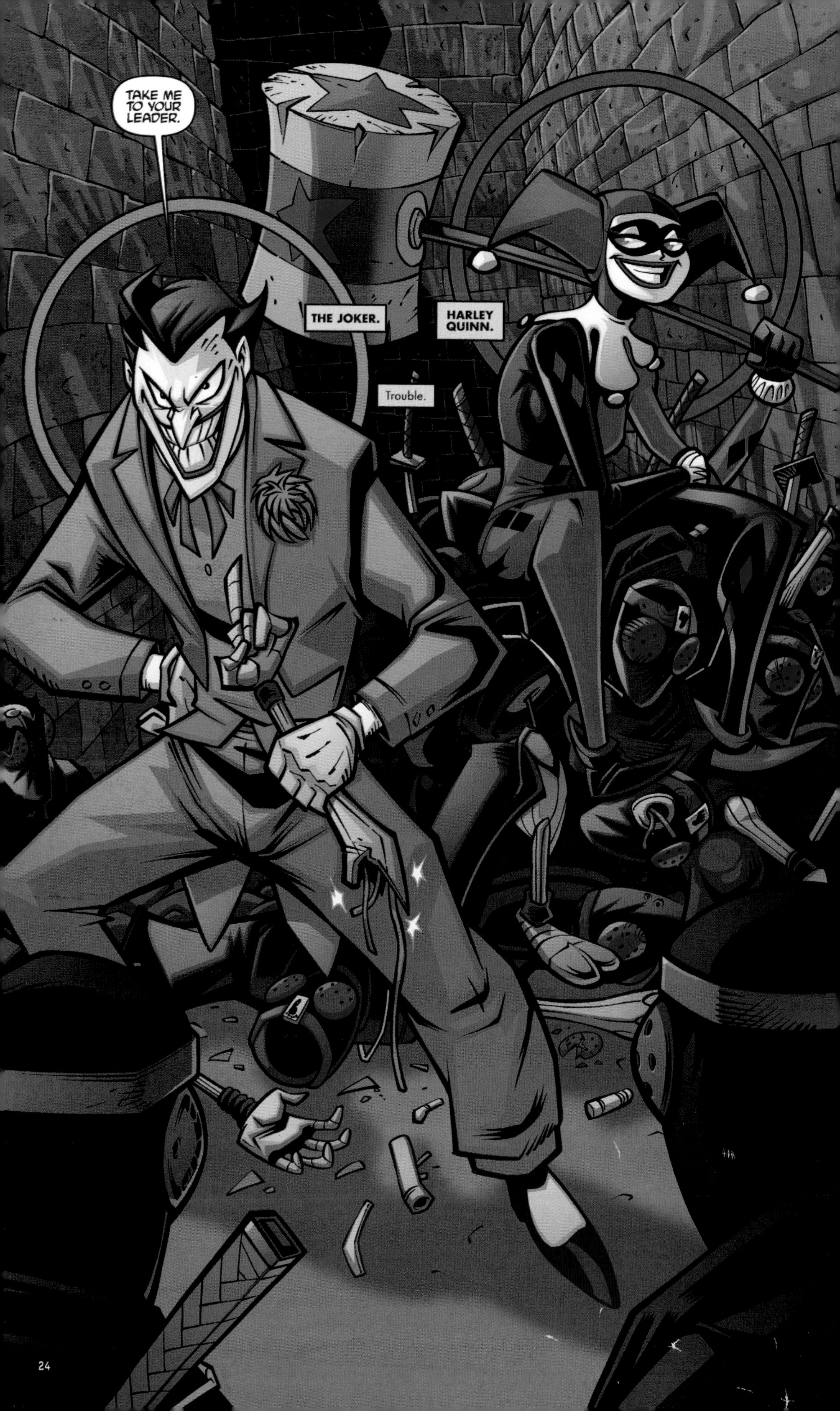
TAKE ME TO YOUR LEADER.
THE JOKER.
HARLEY QUINN.
Trouble.

CREATOR

MATTHEW K. MANNING

THE AUTHOR OF THE AMAZON BEST-SELLING HARDCOVER *BATMAN: A VISUAL HISTORY*, MATTHEW K. MANNING HAS CONTRIBUTED TO MANY COMIC BOOKS, INCLUDING *BEWARE THE BATMAN*, *SPIDER-MAN UNLIMITED*, *PIRATES OF THE CARIBBEAN: SIX SEA SHANTIES*, *JUSTICE LEAGUE ADVENTURES*, *LOONEY TUNES*, AND *SCOOBY-DOO, WHERE ARE YOU?* WHEN NOT WRITING COMICS, MANNING OFTEN AUTHORS BOOKS ABOUT COMICS, AS WELL AS A SERIES OF YOUNG READER BOOKS STARRING SUPERMAN, BATMAN, AND THE FLASH FOR CAPSTONE. HE CURRENTLY RESIDES IN ASHEVILLE, NORTH CAROLINA, WITH HIS WIFE, DOROTHY, AND THEIR TWO DAUGHTERS, LILLIAN AND GWENDOLYN. VISIT HIM ONLINE AT WWW.MATTHEWKMANNING.COM.

JON SOMMARIVA

JON SOMMARIVA WAS BORN IN SYDNEY, AUSTRALIA. HE HAS BEEN DRAWING COMIC BOOKS SINCE 2002. HIS WORK CAN BE SEEN IN *GEMINI*, *REXODUS*, *TMNT ADVENTURES*, AND *STAR WARS ADVENTURES*, AMONG OTHER COMICS. WHEN HE IS NOT DRAWING, HE ENJOYS WATCHING MOVIES AND PLAYING WITH HIS SON, FELIX.

GLOSSARY

asylum (us-SYE-luhm)—a hospital for people who are mentally ill and are unable to live without help

casualty (KAZH-oo-uhl-tee)—a person or thing injured, lost, or destroyed

civilian (si-VIL-yuhn)—a person that is not in the armed services or police force

coordinates (koh-OR-duh-nits)—a set of numbers used to show the position of something on a map

fertilizer (FUHR-tuh-ly-zuhr)—a substance added to soil to make crops grow better

generous (jen-uh-RUSS)—willing to share

inmate (IN-mayts)—a prisoner

portal (POHR-tuhl)—a path between dimensions, worlds, or realms

reinforcements (ree-in-FORSS-muhnts)—extra troops sent into battle

residue (REZ-uh-doo)—what is left after something burns up or evaporates

secrecy (SEE-kri-see)—acting to keep something unknown

security (suh-kuhr-uh-tee)—methods used to protect or keep something in or out

sewer (SOO-ur)—a system, often an underground pipe, that carries away liquid and solid waste

squabbling (SKWAB-ling)—making a noisy argument

trounce (TROUNS)—defeat heavily, crush, or overwhelm

unconscious (uhn-KON-shuhss)—not awake

vengeance (VEN-juhnss)—paying someone back for personal harm

VISUAL QUESTIONS AND WRITING PROMPTS

1. HOW DO YOU KNOW THAT BATMAN AND THE NINJA TURTLES ARE INVESTIGATING THE SAME THING?

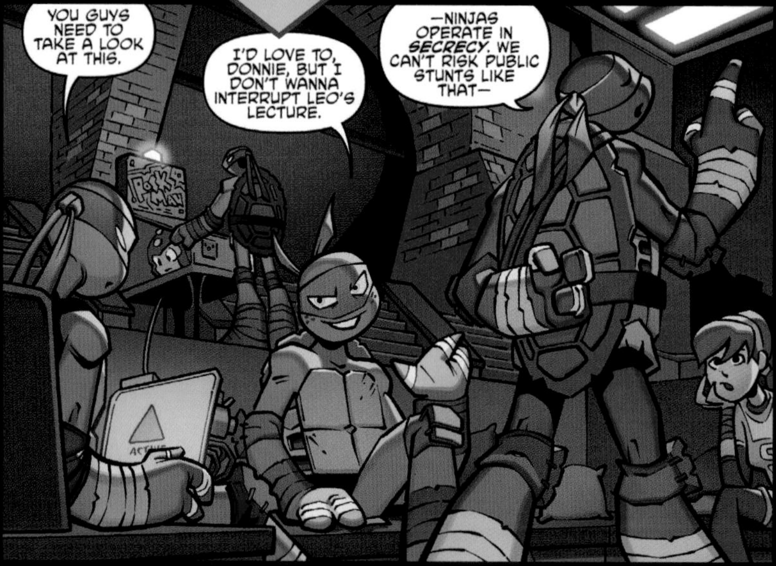

YOU GUYS NEED TO TAKE A LOOK AT THIS.
I'D LOVE TO, DONNIE, BUT I DON'T WANNA INTERRUPT LEO'S LECTURE.
—NINJAS OPERATE IN *SECRECY*. WE CAN'T RISK PUBLIC STUNTS LIKE THAT—

2. HOW CAN YOU TELL THAT THE TURTLE ON THE FAR RIGHT ISN'T MICHELANGELO?

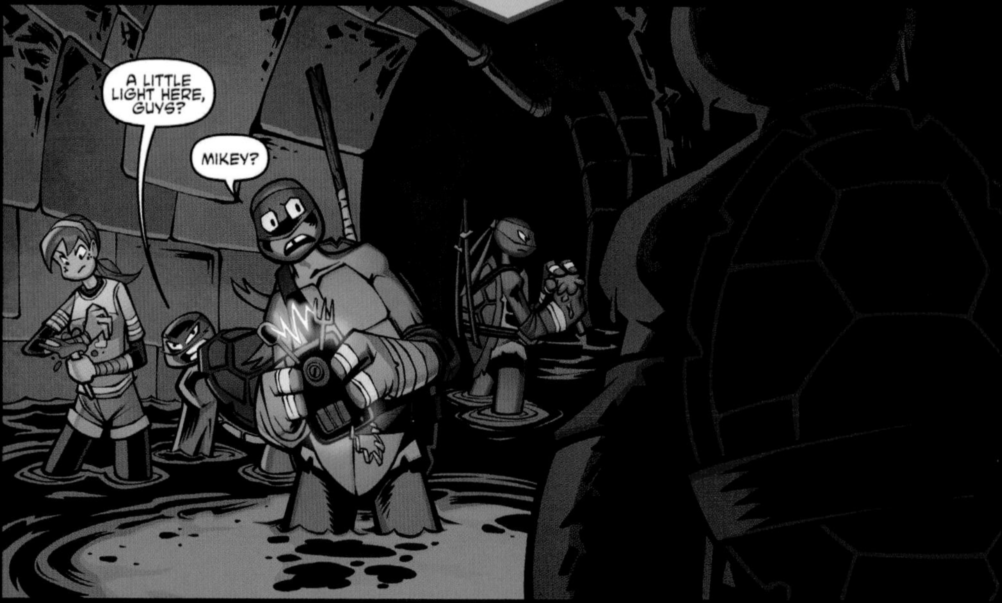

A LITTLE LIGHT HERE, GUYS?
MIKEY?

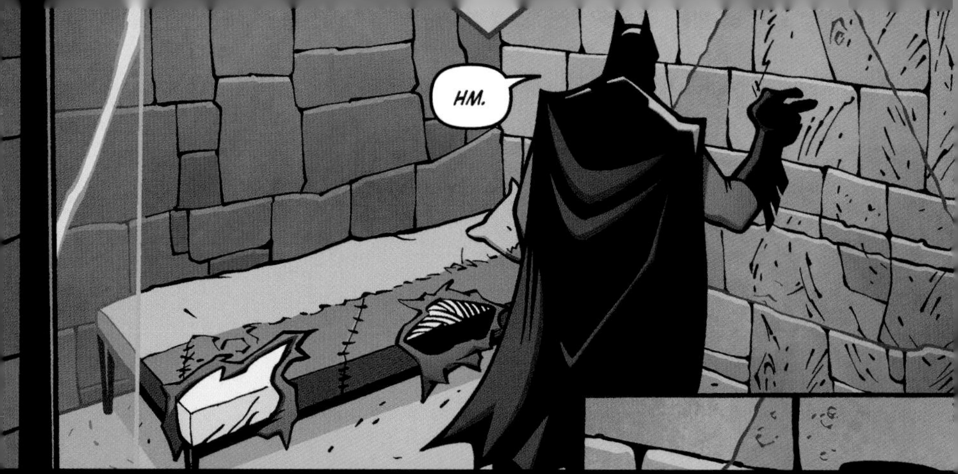
HM.

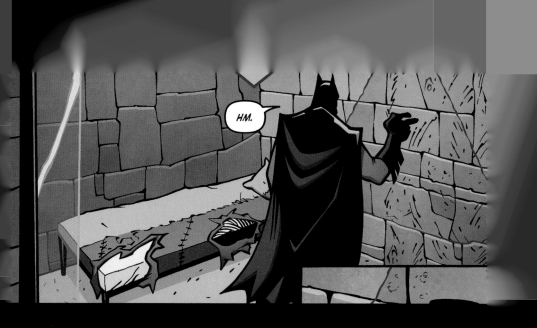

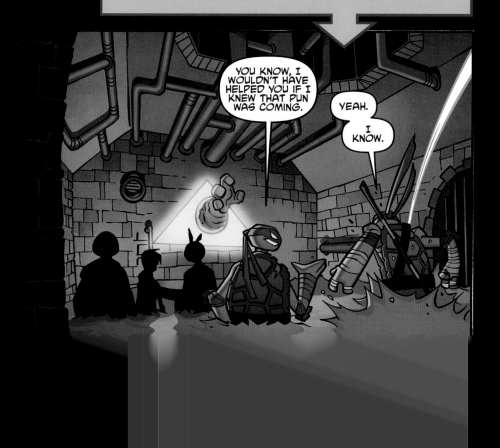

4. WHAT DO YOU THINK HAPPENED TO CLAYFACE AFTER HE WAS PUSHED THROUGH THE PORTAL? WRITE A SCENE DESCRIBING WHERE HE GOES AND WHAT HE DOES NEXT.

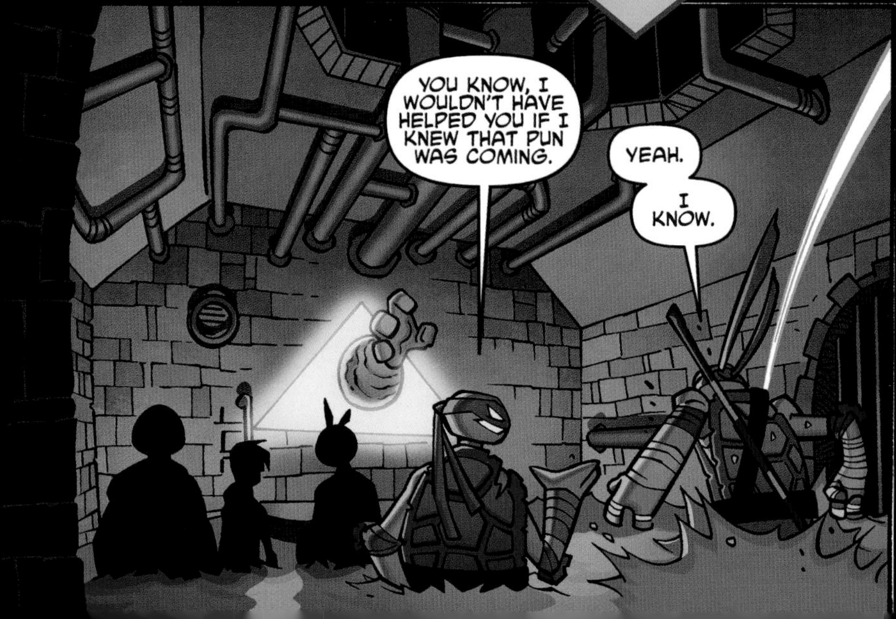
YOU KNOW, I WOULDN'T HAVE HELPED YOU IF I KNEW THAT PUN WAS COMING.
YEAH.
I KNOW.

BATMAN™ TEENAGE MUTANT NINJA TURTLES™
ADVENTURES

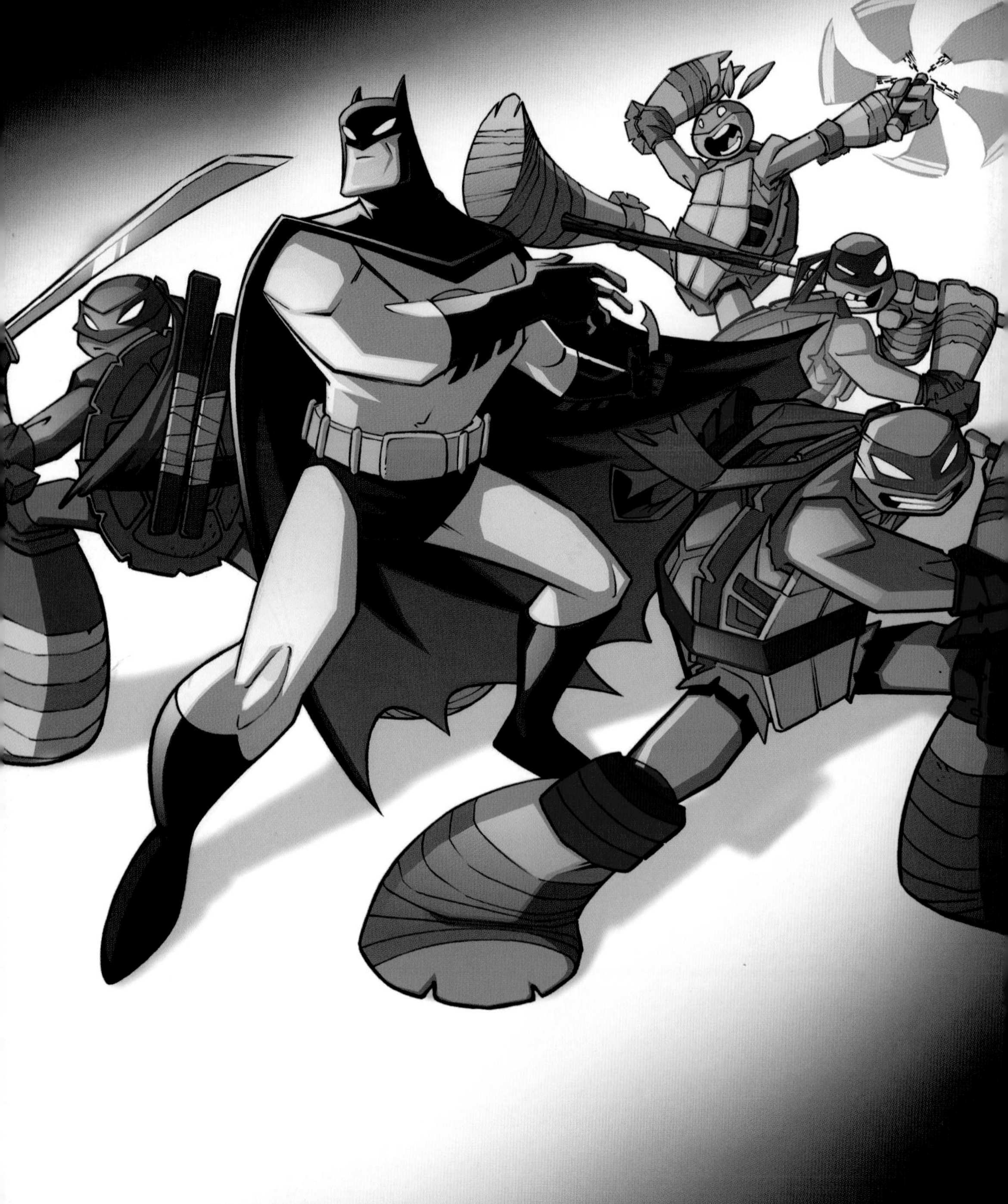

READ THEM ALL!

IDW
DC
BATMAN
TEENAGE MUTANT NINJA TURTLES
ADVENTURES
THE CLOWN AND THE CLAN

IDW
DC
BATMAN
TEENAGE MUTANT NINJA TURTLES
ADVENTURES
GREENER ON THE OTHER SIDE

IDW
DC
BATMAN
TEENAGE MUTANT NINJA TURTLES
ADVENTURES
Manning
Sommariva
Parsons
Ito
THE FACE OF TWO WORLDS

IDW
DC
BATMAN
TEENAGE MUTANT NINJA TURTLES
ADVENTURES
THROUGH THE LOOKING GLASS

IDW
DC
BATMAN
TEENAGE MUTANT NINJA TURTLES
ADVENTURES
THE TERROR OF THE KRAANG

IDW
DC
BATMAN
TEENAGE MUTANT NINJA TURTLES
ADVENTURES
TO LAUGH SO NOT TO CRY

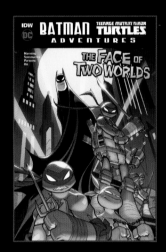

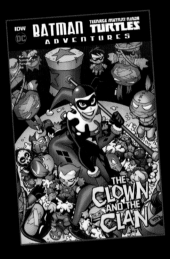

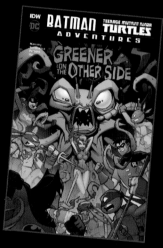

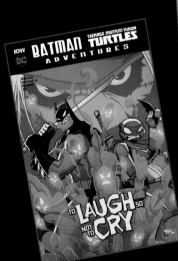

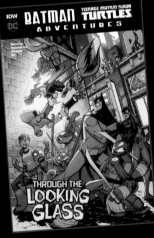

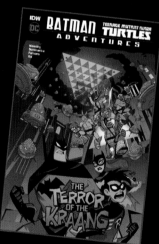

BATMAN

TEENAGE MUTANT NINJA TURTLES

ADVENTURES